THE DREAM DOG

Books by the same author

The Game

My Mother's Daughter

The Time Tree

Twice Times Danger

Wolfsong

For younger readers

Gemma and the Beetle People

The Glass Bird

Kachunka!

The Magic Skateboard

THE DREAM DOG

ENID RICHEMONT

First published 1996 by Walker Books Ltd
87 Vauxhall Walk, London SE11 5HJ

2 4 6 8 10 9 7 5 3 1

This book has been typeset in Sabon.

Printed in England

British Library Cataloguing in Publication Data
A catalogue record for this book is available from
the British Library.

ISBN 0-7445-4130-1

For Alan, Jude and Alfie –
and, of course, Spike!

CHAPTER ONE

He was sad.

The man and the woman didn't seem to understand that.

They thought they could teach him tricks. They thought he'd bark at strangers.

When he cried for his lady, they just got cross.

They kept giving him things he didn't want to eat.

Then they'd go away and leave him for hours and hours...

Josh rode over in the moving van, perched up high in the driver's cabin.

"We might get a dog," he said, "now we've got a house."

The driver grinned. "Your cat wouldn't go for that!"

"It's my sister's cat really," Josh told him.

"Anyway, she wouldn't mind."

"Cats hate moving," said the driver's mate. "Give that animal time to settle down. Then you can start thinking about a dog."

They eased the van in slowly between the parking cones. Josh could look down at the top of Mum's LADYFARE cab.

"Better get started," said the driver, helping him out.

The driver's mate unlocked the back of the van and began to load boxes on to a trolley.

Cath was sitting on the garden wall, drawing faces on her knees with a felt-tip pen. The minute she saw Josh, she stuck out her tongue. "Show-off!" she teased.

The driver's mate came back with the empty trolley. "Fancy a ride?" he offered. Then, "Hang on tight!" he told Cath.

Josh watched as the house filled up with their things – the sofa and the armchairs huddled next to the table, the big mirror and Dad's pictures all bandaged in sacking, three chests of drawers standing round the washing machine, and stacks and stacks of cardboard boxes.

Mum strode over the geranium pots, holding out the cat basket and a packet of crunchies.

"Take Mollie somewhere quiet," she told Josh. "And give her some of these to shut her up. And don't let her out, or she'll be gone in a flash."

"She's not *my* cat," grumbled Josh.

"Don't be difficult," said Mum.

Josh took up the basket and dumped it in Cath's room. Through the bars, Mollie gazed at him with troubled yellow eyes. "Miaow!" she wailed. "Miaow!"

Josh shook out some crunchies and the wailing stopped. "You're Cath's, really," he said, stroking the marmalade smudge between her black and brown ears. "It was Cath who found you." It wasn't fair, he thought. He'd have liked a cat, too, but pets weren't allowed where they'd lived before. Then the caretaker'd gone all goo-goo over Cath and the kitten. Just this once, she'd said. Since you're moving. As long as it's house-trained...

The men came upstairs, heaving one of the bunk beds. Cath came dancing after them, being bossy.

"I want it *here*," she said. Then she changed her mind. "No, under the window so I can look out." She bounced on the mattress, stood up, then frowned. "But I want my *desk* here, don't I?"

"You haven't got a desk," Josh pointed out.

"No, but I'm having one." Cath turned to the moving men. "Can you put my bed back in the corner?"

The moving men teased her. "That'll be an extra fifty quid."

The last box was unloaded. The van was empty. The men folded up their blankets and got ready to go.

"I'll make us some tea," offered Mum.

"No gas yet," they reminded her.

"Ah! We've got an electric kettle." Mum grinned.

Cath brought down the cat basket. Mollie stepped out cautiously. Everything was in the wrong place, and the wrong place smelt funny.

Dad opened a tin of cat food and spooned some into a bowl. "It's OK, Mollie," he said, but she glared at him, then fled.

They sent out for pizzas, and ate them in the garden.

The lady next door looked over the fence. She had brushy blonde hair and big dangly earrings.

"You could have had a bite to eat with us." She smiled. "Nice to have someone in that empty house at last."

A girl of about Cath's age popped up beside her. "Hi," she said, looking curiously at Cath.

Mollie appeared from nowhere, stepping delicately through the grass.

"Mollie's found the cat door," grinned Dad.

"You mean, *dog* door," corrected Mum. "That hole's too big for a cat."

"Great," said Josh. "Then we won't have to make one."

"We're not having a dog," declared Cath firmly. "A dog would chase my cat."
"Our cat," Dad reminded her.
"I found her," crowed Cath.
"Show-off!" growled Josh.

CHAPTER TWO

He kept thinking about home, the way it smelt, the way it felt. Locked up here, in this sky place, there wasn't much else to do.

Then something strange suddenly happened – a dream that wasn't quite a dream.

He'd closed his eyes as usual and made pictures in his head. The nice, chewy ball that he'd lost in the brambles. His warm, bobbly blanket, and the cat-smell place on his lady's bedside rug, where he'd worried at the threads until he'd made a little hole.

And all at once, something called, and he was there, in her room...

Josh found it funny to sleep at floor level, strange not having someone creaking about below.

"We could always put the bunk beds back together," Mum said, "until you both get used to things."

But they'd already agreed. "We want to sleep in our own rooms," said Josh.

It was just past sunset when they'd gone up. For a while, they'd stayed awake, sorting out their things, and chatting to each other through the wall.

"Josh?"

"What?"

"I've got your animals book."

"That's OK."

"Josh?"

"What?"

"I've got Mollie, too. She's purring."

"Great," Josh said. "That means she's settling down."

Then he'd gone off to sleep and woken up thirsty. He reached out for the lamp switch but there wasn't any lamp, and the bare window drew black lines across the floorboards, and a half-moon glimmered, then faded behind cloud. The room smelt funny, fusty – not a bit like the flat. A single spike of creeper *tap-tap*ped against the glass.

"Hey, Cath?" whispered Josh, forgetting she wasn't sleeping below.

He got out of bed and switched on the light – a single bulb that swung from the middle of the ceiling. Then he went to the bathroom and took a long drink, letting water from the tap run all over his face.

It would be OK tomorrow, he thought, getting back into bed. He'd find his old lamp, for starters, then sort out the rest of his stuff. *His* room, he reminded himself. No more bossy little sister to interfere.

And there *would* be a dog one day, no matter what Cath said. It made sense, didn't it? You got a flat. Then a cat. Then a house. Then a dog. And Mum couldn't go on saying that there wasn't enough space. They had a garden now, didn't they? And a park just up the road.

Josh lay, gazing at the squiggles on the wallpaper. He could put the light out later, he thought. Anyway, it wouldn't have felt so creepy if he'd had a dog.

But what kind of a dog? He could never make up his mind.

A black and white collie would be nice, he thought. Like the ones Grammie had.

Or a golden retriever. Or a Labrador...

Its eyebrow tufts came first.

Then a faint stripe like a painted white frown that dissolved into the grey whiskers that sprang from its nose.

Then a whole dog was sitting beside his bed.

Josh rubbed his eyes. I'm dreaming you, he thought.

But moths went on dancing around the bare light-bulb, and the dog went on sitting there, watching his face.

"You're funny," Josh giggled, holding out his hand. "You're like a funny old man..." He reached out to stroke it, but his hand went right through. Weird, thought Josh. You can always touch things in dreams.

The dog's silly eyebrows seemed to arch pathetically. *I want you to like me*, they seemed to say.

"I do like you," Josh told it. "But I wish I could stroke you." He yawned. "Anyway, I'm having a Labrador..."

Mum left long before Josh woke up.

They helped Dad with the breakfast things, then they started on their rooms.

"I want shelves here," Cath said. "Can I?"

Dad banged at the wall. "Seems solid enough."

"Will you paint me something?" begged Cath. "Like a jungle? Or mountains?"

"You seem to be doing all right yourself," said Dad.

"But you're an artist," grumbled Cath. "You can make things look real."

"Who wants real things," asked Dad, "when you draw cars as nice as this?"

"Come and see what I've done," pleaded Josh. (Drawing on wallpaper had felt really wicked.)

"We know, we know." Cath skipped after

him. "Boring old dogs."

"Got you!" Josh pointed. "See? That's Batman."

"And that's the gasman," said Dad, belting off downstairs.

CHAPTER THREE

He'd cried when they put his lady in the big white van. She'd never have left him. He knew that.

His bowl had kept on filling, but he was never really hungry.

He'd watched.

And he'd waited.

He knew she'd come back.

One by one the cats left. Well, he'd never really liked them.

He went on watching. And waiting.

Then the man and woman came.

By the end of the week, everything that mattered was in its place. They could fry chips in the kitchen. They could switch on the microwave. Dad could run the washing machine, and all of Josh's dinosaur models were standing on a shelf.

At the weekend, they hired a sanding machine. When it was Dad's turn to use it, Mum ran outside.

The man next door was clipping some roses.

"Sounds like World War Three," he grumbled.

"Sorry," Mum said.

The blonde lady on the other side looked over the fence.

"We're off to the beach!" she yelled. "To get away from all that din. Why don't I take your two with us?"

"Yes, please!" shouted Cath.

They packed a football and a Frisbee and swimming things and towels. Mum gave them some spending money, then they piled into the car. The girls chattered on the back seat, but Josh had to sit in front with the lady next door.

"Have a good time!" called Mum.

"You bet!" yelled Cath.

The lady next door brought out a big bag of sweets.

"Have one," she said.

Josh took one. "Thanks."

"My name's Pat," said the lady next door. "You call me Pat."

Josh wriggled, feeling silly.

"OK," he mumbled.

"Like your new house?"

"It's all right..."

"Prefer your old place?"

He thought about it. "Not really. This house is big. We can have our own rooms."

"But?"

"All my friends are back there," blurted Josh.

"They can get on the bus," Pat pointed out. "Anyway, you two'll make lots of new friends up at Amy's school."

They parked the car and scrambled up a grassy bank, then scrunched across a long pebbly beach.

Josh dug out a hollow and made them a base.

"Great," said Pat. "It's like having a windbreak."

They bought candyfloss and crisps and splashed about in the sea. The two girls fooled around, playing some private game.

Pat scooped up water and threw it over Josh.

"Hey!" squealed Josh, shaking himself. Then he splashed her right back.

"I'm having a horse," announced Cath on the way home.

Pat laughed. "Isn't your garden a bit small for that?"

"She doesn't mean in the garden," said Amy. "You can get shares in a pony. It lives in a stable, but it's still partly yours, and you can go and visit it whenever you like."

"I'm getting a dog," said Josh.

"No, you're not," said Cath.

"The old lady who lived in your house had a dog," Pat told them. "Miss Nelson..." She sighed. "Broke his little heart when she died. Never saw a dog so sad."

They parked behind Mum's cab.

Then they all went inside to admire the newly sanded floor.

"It's a lovely job," said Pat, "but you two must be exhausted."

"No one's cooking tonight," Mum told her. "It's a take-away for us."

"Oh, forget it," said Pat. "Come round later for a barbecue. Nothing fancy. Just sausages and buns."

At sunset, the barbecue was glowing red. Pat's sausages sizzled and spat, and the potatoes were crumbly inside their crackly skins. They ate them with butter and cheese, blowing on their fingers, and slurping up icy mouthfuls of fizzy drink.

Cath and Amy took turns on the swing. Pat watched them and smiled. "Cath was just what Amy needed."

Josh suddenly felt old and very lonely. He'd been stuck with a grown-up all day, and it wasn't much fun.

"Stop hogging that swing!" bellowed Pat.

"Let Josh have a go!"

"OK," said Amy. "Come on," she offered. "Give you a push."

The swing squeak-squeaked as it rose and fell, and the garden smelt sweetly of warm grass and cooking.

And stars whizzed through the leaves above Josh's head. There was a dog star up there somewhere. He'd read it in a book.

I wish for a dog, he told it silently.

It was silly, but anything was worth a try...

CHAPTER FOUR

The man and woman yelled at him for messing on their carpet.

He wouldn't have done that at his lady's place, but then her place was home.

He closed his eyes and began to remember.

He remembered his rug, the way the threads tickled his nose and made him sneeze. Then something called out to him again and suddenly there he was.

He knew it was home, even though it looked funny.

All his lady's things had gone. And there was that boy again.

He was a nice boy. He liked him.

But why was the boy sleeping in his lady's room?

Things were getting better, Josh thought when he went to bed that night. Pat next door was so nice, and even Amy wasn't bad. And his room was beginning to look like his. There were puzzles and games and books stacked against the wall. He'd put up his 3-D wallchart and his dinosaurs poster, and Mum had wired up his lamp so he could read in bed.

He opened up his dog book and settled down to choose. He'd made a wish, he remembered, grinning, so he'd better be prepared.

But his throat felt smoky, and his tummy felt bubbly, and his eyes kept stinging and wanting to close. He slept sitting up, then something disturbed him.

Silly, he thought. He hadn't turned off the light.

His hand was on the switch when something made him turn. The dog from his dream was sitting beside the bed, its front paws stretched out, and its sorrowful eyes fixed on Josh's face.

Josh blinked.

"You can't be my wish," he muttered. "I mean, wishes don't work. Anyway, I really meant a Labrador or something. But you're OK. You're nice." He slithered out of bed and held out his hand. "Come on then, boy," he called, but the dog drew back.

Perhaps it was scared, Josh thought, of being in a new place. Just like Mollie'd been.

"Stay!" he told it.

He crept downstairs. Mum and Dad were in the back room, watching television. He tiptoed into the kitchen and shook out some cat crunchies.

Mollie came and sniffed at them.

"No, not for you," said Josh.

He went back up. "Got something nice," he told his dog, but the room was empty.

He looked under the bed and inside the cupboard. He checked in the bathroom, and even the loo. Then he went into Cath's room. He could hear her snoring. He switched on the light and she woke up.

"What are you doing?" she asked.

"Looking for something."

"Go back to sleep," mumbled Cath.

"It's not here anyway," said Josh.

It all felt like a dream until he went down for breakfast. Everyone was outside, sitting on the grass.

Cath glared at him. "You woke me up in the middle of the night."

Josh squirmed. "I was looking for something."

"Did you find it?" asked Dad.

"Couldn't it wait?" Mum said.

The telephone rang. It was Josh's friend Damien. "Can I come over," he asked Josh, "with my brother this afternoon?"

They turned up just after three, with hurley sticks.

"Show us your room," said Damien. "And

the garden and all. Is it big enough for hurling?"

Dad laughed. "You'd lose the ball in that jungle!"

Josh showed them round, then they went upstairs.

"So when are you getting that dog?" Damien asked.

"Soon," said Josh vaguely. "When we've sorted things out."

They played a bit with models and magic tricks while Damien's brother, Greg, flipped through some of Josh's comics.

"You been back to Ireland yet," he asked, "to see your grammie?"

"We can't this year," said Josh. "Too much to do."

Damien was getting restless. "You said there was a park."

"Victoria Park," said Josh. "Just up the road."

"Can we go?" asked Damien.

"OK," agreed Josh, and they clattered downstairs.

"We're going to the park," Greg said. "For hurling practice."

"Take your shin guards," said Mum.

"No need," Damien told her. "We're just playing with tennis balls."

"Not much of a game," Mum sniffed, "with only the three of you." She grinned. "Why don't we all go? I'm a great one for the hurling. We could have two against two, and take it in turns."

"I'll drop out first," offered Dad.

They walked up to the park. Dad sat under a tree and began to draw. After a while, Greg came over to look.

"They're just squiggles," he said, and went back to the game.

Josh changed places with Cath, and squatted down beside Dad. They were quiet together. Josh liked watching Dad work.

"Dad?" he asked at last, because he really had to know. "Can dogs have ghosts?"

Dad stopped drawing and stared at him. "What a question! Why?"

"Because there was this dog. In my room." Josh went pink, feeling silly. "But when I went to get it some crunchies, it had gone."

"When was this?" asked Dad, sharpening his pencil.

"Last night," admitted Josh.

"After all you ate at Pat's?" Dad grinned. "No wonder you had funny dreams."

"It wasn't a dream," insisted Josh. "I went looking for it. Cath saw me."

"Then you sleepwalked," Dad told him. "It happens sometimes."

CHAPTER FIVE

The man and woman's place was high. It hung in the sky.

Its tiny yard had railings and plants in pots.

There was no grass to run through, no smell trails to follow. And the inside smells were always the same.

The rooms smelt of spicy stuff and flowery stuff and bath. But his new basket smelt of nothing, and he longed for his old one.

He tried out the smooth sofa that smelt of skin, but they shouted and slapped him. Oh, where was his lady?

He closed his eyes and made a picture – white fur on her head and silver circles round her eyes, a glittery thing on her finger, feet-smelling slippers on a stool.

Maybe this time she'd be there.

He remembered her armchair with its rough old blanket, the chocolate drops she used to give him for being a good boy. He remembered lying at her feet, watching the fire that hissed and whispered and toasted his nose...

Dad hung a NO ENTRY sign on the front room door.

"And that means *you*," he warned Mollie.

Cath and Josh peered through the window for a while, watching him varnish the pale floorboards to a glistening golden brown. Then they went back to the garden to finish their game.

At the end of the morning, Dad cleaned up.

"Come and help with lunch!" he called, dabbling the varnish brush in a tin of white spirit.

"Pooh!" complained Cath, holding her nose.

"When can we put all the stuff back?" asked Josh. "It's like we've just moved in all over again."

"Not for a week or so," said Dad. "It'll need a second coat, at least. And then we'll have to start on the other room."

"I prefer carpet," said Cath, bringing out some cheese. "Everyone else has got carpet."

"Well, we're going to have rugs," Dad told her. "And beautiful floors."

After lunch, Amy brought a friend round to play with Cath, and Dad went upstairs to work in his studio.

Josh went up to his room and drew on the wallpaper, adding bits to his Batman picture, and listening to the three girls fooling about.

After a while, he went down and rang Damien, but Damien was out with some other boys. Josh messed round in the garden, kicking a ball.

It was easy for Cath, he thought. Girls made friends so quickly. But you always had someone to play with if you had a dog...

Cath and Amy and the other girl took over the garden. Josh went back in and poured himself some juice. Then he *ran* up to Dad's studio.

"Not *now*," growled Dad.

Mum came home. She'd just picked up the shopping.

"Josh!" she shouted. "Help me unload!"

Grown-ups might sometimes say *please*, thought Josh.

And he hoped Mum wouldn't turn up at the new school in her cab. It had been bad enough before.

"Josh's taxi's arrived," Miss Turner had joked, and they'd teased him for weeks. "Taxi! Taxi!" they'd yell.

It was always the same ones, the ones who'd got at Damien. "Thick Mick," they'd call Damien. "Got any bombs?"

One day, Josh told Damien that his mum

was Irish. That was the day they'd started being friends.

"How's the front room floor?" asked Mum vaguely.

"I'll go and see," offered Josh.

He peeped round the door. Curled up on the gleaming varnish, staring at the old hearth, lay his dog.

Josh was horrified. "Get out!" he yelled. "My dad'll kill you!" But the dog just went on lying there.

Josh lunged forward, trying to grab it, but it stretched its front paws sleepily, and began thumping its tail.

Mollie ran in between Josh's feet, then she high-stepped stickily across the floor. Something interesting was going on, and she had to find out what.

Suddenly she froze. Then she hissed and backed off, pressing a little trail of paw marks into the smooth golden floor.

Dad was coming down to say hello to Mum just as Mollie scrabbled out, her fur fluffed up and furious.

"Who opened that door?" Dad shouted. Then he saw Josh. "Come out of there!" he roared. He crouched to check on his floor. "A whole morning's work wasted!" he raged.

"It was that dog again," wailed Josh.

"What dog?" asked Mum.

"Dad knows," sniffled Josh.
"Oh, Josh," sighed Dad.

Josh lay awake that night, trying to work it out.

Sometimes people want a thing so badly, Dad had told him, that they think it's really there.

But it *had* been there, thought Josh. It had even upset Mollie.

Cats saw things sometimes that people couldn't see. Even back in the flat, Mollie would stiffen suddenly, and stare. "She's seeing *gho-o-sts*," they used to say, putting on wobbly voices.

But Mollie had seen that dog, and then that dog had vanished. There'd been no marks left where he'd sat, no dog hairs stuck to the floor.

No dog hairs. No paw marks.

But a ghost? In the middle of the afternoon?

The ghost of a dog?

But why shouldn't a dog turn into a ghost?

It had to be a dead dog first, Josh remembered. He shivered. That was creepy. It was a nice dog. He liked it. He didn't want it to be dead.

The wish had gone all wrong.

He didn't want a ghost dog.

Who wanted a ghost dog you couldn't even touch when you could have a real dog you could play with and take for walks?

CHAPTER SIX

Everyone seemed to be cross with him.

Even the boy.

People went crazy sometimes, all dogs knew that.

But why was home so different?

He tried to understand.

These were new people. New people in his lady's house. (Oh, where was his lady?)

But these were shadow people you couldn't touch. Even that show-off cat was just a shadow.

The boy was nice. The boy was special.

But whenever the dog tried to touch him, his paws went right through.

Big clouds billowed, and a cool wind whipped up a scuttering of dry leaves.

Dad had scythed the long grass, and raked it up in a hay pile. "We need a rabbit," he joked.

"We need a horse," said Cath firmly. "But a rabbit would do."

They found blackberries and raspberries in the overgrown bushes. Then Pat came round with apples. "We always have too many," she said, "so I give them away."

Josh suddenly thought of something.

"You know that old lady who used to live in our house?"

"Miss Nelson?"

Josh nodded. "Did her dog die, too?"

Pat frowned, remembering.

"No," she said. "But he pined... We all fed him for a while, but he didn't eat much. Too miserable. Missed her. Then a couple of her relatives turned up and took him back with them. A stuck-up pair." She pulled a face. "Never thought they'd bother. Still, you can never tell. Probably spoilt him rotten..."

So the ghost dog couldn't be *that* dog, thought Josh.

"What did her dog look like?" he asked.

Pat grinned. "Funny-looking mutt. Another stray, someone told me. Like her cats. She took it in when it was a pup, and it fair wore her out. But then, old Miss Nelson was always a softie."

"But what did it look like?" persisted Josh. (Sometimes grown-ups were so dumb.)

"Oh, you know," said Pat. "A mongrel. Silly face." She giggled. "Always looked surprised..."

That afternoon, Josh rode over to Damien's on the bus.

He ran up five flights of stairs, then rang the bell.

Inside, the boys were watching a horror movie while their mum did the ironing and their little sister, Maura, threw things out of her playpen.

Josh and Damien hung about, then they went to Damien's room.

"Do you believe in things like that?" asked Josh. "I mean, vampires and stuff?"

"The films are stupid," said Damien. "All that blood comes out of bottles. And anyone can buy vampire teeth." He put some in and pulled a face. "Watch out! I'll get you!"

They fooled around for a bit, attacking each other.

"What about ghosts, though?" asked Josh.

"I believe in *banshees*," said Damien. "I know someone who's heard one."

"We've got a ghost," said Josh. "In that house."

Damien looked impressed. "You having me on?"

Josh took a deep breath. "It's a dog."

"What's a dog?" asked Damien.

"The ghost," said Josh. "It's a dog."

Damien fell about, laughing. "You can't have a ghost that's a dog!"

"Why not?" asked Josh.

"You've got to have a soul to turn into a ghost," Damien told him. "Sure, everyone knows that."

Dogs have souls, thought Josh, but he didn't want a fight.

They began to talk about other things – about Damien's new teacher, about the Irish Club, about people they both knew at Peterston Junior.

And Josh felt sad again, because he wouldn't be there.

Mum turned up early to collect him, then she sat chatting with Damien's mum.

"We'll have a party," she promised, "when we've finished sorting out the house."

"Will you have your dog by then?" asked Damien.

"Don't encourage him," sighed Mum.

"Will you *ever* let me have a dog?" grumbled Josh on the way home.

"You and your dog..." Mum shook her head. "You'll be starting the new school next week. One thing at a time."

It wasn't ever going to happen, Josh thought in bed that night.

They'd go on putting it off until he was grown up.

Then he'd get himself a dog. Maybe two, or even three.

He put out his light and snuggled down, but

the dark felt scary, and the creeper rattled and tapped against the window-pane.

It could be a vampire, trying to get in.

He went off to sleep, but the vampire came after him. It had bloodshot eyeballs and long, pointed teeth. It came closer and closer. Its black wings spread out.

"Aaah!" screamed Josh, and snapped himself awake.

He switched on the light and there was his dog, lying across the foot of his bed.

He pushed up his feet, feeling the featherweight of the duvet. There was really nothing there.

And yet the dog's chestnut eyes went on watching him. Are you still cross with me? they seemed to ask.

Josh reached out, longing to stroke him, and sad that he couldn't.

Then he curled up, feeling safe, and went back to sleep.

CHAPTER SEVEN

Every evening, after six, the man and woman would take him out.

The three of them would ride down, down, down in the little room that moved.

Then they'd walk to the park. The woman would clip-clop, clip-clop, clip-clop.

They'd turn him loose to do his business. Then they'd clamp him on the lead.

Running, he remembered. Wind in your ears and your legs flying... His lady used to sit and throw him a ball.

Home, he thought.

But his lady had gone.

Even the shadow boy went away now, but he came back. Every day. At the same time. The end of the afternoon.

He picked up the boy's new pattern and began to look out for him...

* * *

On Tuesday, Mum arranged a late shift and took Josh and Cath to school.

She parked the LADYFARE cab in a side street. Josh hoped no one would notice.

They walked across the playground and into the office. The school secretary got up. "Hello, you two," she smiled.

Their teachers came to collect them. Cath went skipping after hers.

Josh's teacher pushed open a door. "Quiet!" she called, then, "This is Josh," she said.

She found him a place next to a boy called Matthew. Josh looked round at all the unfamiliar faces and wished he was back in his old school, with Damien, where even the people who teased him he knew.

Outside, in the playground, they started to ask him questions.

"Where did you go to school before?"

"Peterston Juniors."

"We beat them at football," someone said.

"Where d'you live now?"

"Albert Road," said Josh.

"We live just round the corner," said Matthew. "In one of those flats."

Dad came round at half past three.

"How did it go?" he asked.

"Great!" shouted Cath.

"It was OK," Josh said.

Amy called out, " 'Bye, Cath!" and went off

with her gran.

"So you girls are in the same class," said Dad. "Aren't you lucky?"

Cath always was, thought Josh. She was the one who'd found the kitten. And she always made friends. Maybe girls were nicer. No one ever seemed to think of yelling "Taxi!" after Cath.

But now he had something Cath didn't have. No one else had a ghost dog. And it had chosen him.

He began wondering what to call it. It had to have a name. It had a collar, he remembered. So it must have had a name when it was alive (and even thinking things like that made Josh feel sad).

He began to stay awake at night, waiting up for it. Would it come slowly, like smoke? Or would it suddenly *be* there?

But he never saw it come, and he always got sleepy. Then he'd wake up from some dream, and there it would be.

He thought of telling Mum, or Cath, but even Dad hadn't believed him, and Damien was so sure dogs couldn't have ghosts...

School started to take up a lot of Josh's time. He began to learn people's names. His teacher was Miss Thompson. She wasn't so bad.

The leaves turned gold and red and russet. Spiders' webs hung silver on the bushes in the garden. It would be his birthday soon, Josh thought. His first birthday in the new house.

One day, Matthew asked him round to play after school.

"It's just up the road," Josh told Dad, "so I can bring myself home."

Matthew had guinea-pigs in a cage on the balcony. They looked a bit like fat little dogs, Josh thought.

"You got any pets?" Matthew asked him.

"We've got a cat," said Josh. He was about to say, And we might be getting a dog, when he stopped himself, and thought.

He already had a dog. His wish dog. The ghost dog. If they let him have a real dog, it might feel left out.

But the ghost dog wasn't true, he knew that really. It was probably just like Dad said – he'd wanted a dog so badly that he'd just made one up.

A guinea-pig might be nice. You could play with a guinea-pig. But it wouldn't chase sticks and come and lick your hand. He thought of Grammie's two big collies on the farm in County Clare. Those two would even swim with you, their heads bobbing up and down in the brown waters of the loch.

Matthew turned on the TV and they watched for a while. Then Matthew's mum said, "Goodness, Josh! It's nearly seven.

You'd better be going home."

Josh ran up the street and round the corner, and there, outside the front gate, stood his dog.

Mum came charging out of the house, her car keys jingling.

"You're late," she called. She ran right through the ghost dog.

"No!" yelled Josh.

"Yes, you are," grinned Mum, unlocking the cab. Josh stood there, gaping.

Then Mum ran up to him and gave him a hug.

"Have a nice time?"

He nodded, looking anxiously past her shoulder.

The dog wagged its tail, and then it was gone.

CHAPTER EIGHT

His lady wasn't coming back.

He'd really known it all the time.

One day, she'd smelt wrong, she'd felt wrong. He'd tried to make her better, but she'd been so very tired...

And now the shadow people were living in her house. She'd have liked the shadow cat. She'd have liked the boy.

It was still home, and he longed to be there.

He could find his way back, if only he was free.

But he wasn't free.

He began to be naughty. Very naughty.

He ate all the leaves off the plants in the pots, then sicked them up on the pale grey carpet.

He shredded the woman's silk scarf, then gnawed a hole in the smooth skin sofa.

Once, he stole the man's sausage from his

breakfast plate.

They screamed and they shouted. Then he cowered.

Didn't they understand? He didn't want to be there.

He wanted them to take him home...

"You look as if you've just seen a ghost," said Dad.

"I have," Josh told him.

"Had a good time at Matthew's?"

"He's got guinea-pigs," said Josh. "He might give me one."

" 'Thought you wanted a dog."

"Guinea-pigs are OK."

Josh took an apple and went upstairs. Cath was drawing on the wallpaper – a rainbow helicopter with red and purple rotors. Josh curled up on her bed and began munching his apple.

"You know ghosts?" he said at last.

Cath went on drawing.

"If you walked right through one," said Josh, "do you think it would hurt?"

Cath looked at him scornfully. " 'Course it wouldn't, stupid." She had a streak of purple across one cheek. "Ghosts can't hurt you," she said, "because they're not really there."

But Josh had been thinking of it the other way round – the way Mum had gone marching right through the middle of the ghost dog, the way the dog had gazed at him, then wagged its tail and vanished.

Maybe she'd broken something.

Maybe it wouldn't come back.

Josh waited up that night, worrying about the ghost dog. He even heard Mum coming in, long after Dad had gone to bed.

He tried to think up names for it, even tried calling it. "Hey, Sam? Kelly? Buster? You OK, boy?"

And then suddenly it was morning, and time for school.

They were doing a project on the family. Grans and grandpas. Aunties and uncles. Sisters and brothers and mums and dads.

Josh drew a big family tree, with Mollie at the bottom. Then he put in Grammie O'Keefe and Gran and Grandpa Roberts, and Auntie Maeve in Ireland, and Uncle Jim in Hull. He put in Mum with her clipped red hair and freckles, and Dad in his paint-stained T-shirt and Cath with her pink hair clips, and then himself.

"Now we're going to write something about each person," said Miss Thompson. "Even cats and dogs and gerbils. They've got stories, too."

Josh started with Mollie. She had a story.

That made him think about his ghost dog, and it made him feel sad. He knew nothing about him, except that he was dead...

He started writing.

Gran and Grandpa Roberts live in Brighton and they've got one black cat, one black and white cat and one ginger cat.

Grammie O'Keefe lives on a farm in Ireland and she's got two collies called Sam and Kelly.

My dad's an artist. He does pictures for books.

Miss Thompson looked over his shoulder.

"Lucky boy," she said. "Would your dad come in and talk to us one day?"

Matthew walked home with them that afternoon.

The house was looking good now, with bright coloured rugs on the glossy floorboards, and some of Dad's pictures hanging on the walls.

Matthew tickled Mollie's tummy.

"Where's your mum?" he asked.

"Working." Then Josh said it. "She's a taxi driver."

Matthew goggled. "Taxi drivers are men."

"Not all of them," said Cath, joining in.

"Do you go for rides in her taxi?"

"Sometimes," said Josh.

"Wow!" Matthew said. "My mum can't even drive."

They went out to the garden to fly Matthew's mini-Frisbee. They flew it over the fence, but Amy sent it back. Then Josh sent it spinning into the brambles.

"Some shot!" grumbled Matthew.

"The wind got it," said Josh.

Matthew forced his way in and reached out for the Frisbee. "Ouch! It's prickly," he grumbled. "Hey, there's an old ball in here," he yelled, throwing it out.

Josh picked it up. It was pockmarked and scarred with damp green moss.

He dropped it, and suddenly the ghost dog was there.

Josh picked up the ball. He couldn't help doing it. The dog watched him expectantly.

"Catch!" called Matthew. The Frisbee whizzed past Josh's ear and bounced off the kitchen window. "You asleep?" shouted Matthew.

Then Josh blinked.

The dog was gone.

CHAPTER NINE

They spread newspapers on the kitchen floor and shut him up inside. Can't do much damage in there, they told him.

He gnawed miserably at the edges of his nice clean basket. That boy had found his ball, the one his lady'd given him.

Now he had to get out.

He had to find his way home...

"We'll give a house-warming party," said Mum. "Next Saturday."

They asked Damien's lot, and Pat and Amy next door.

"Can Matthew come?" asked Josh.

"Sure he can." Mum frowned. "Listen. I found a filthy old ball in your room. You can't want it. It's full of holes."

"You haven't thrown it away?" asked Josh anxiously.

"I'd like to," said Mum. "But I didn't."

Josh went to check. Mum had cleaned off the moss, and had stood the ball on an old plastic bag.

Josh picked it up and turned it over in his hands, and once again felt the closeness of the ghost dog. He'd known all the time that the ball belonged to him.

Perhaps the old lady's dog *had* died after all. Hadn't Pat said that thing about it breaking its heart? Could you really die of sadness? Josh wondered.

And each day, when they got home from school, the dog would be waiting.

Josh wanted to call it, Here, boy! Good dog!, but Cath was always with him and she'd think he was nuts.

"Don't step on that bit of pavement," he'd say.

"Why not?" Cath would ask, barging through the dog.

But it didn't seem to mind. It didn't seem to notice. It just looked at Josh and wagged its tail, and then it was gone.

At school, they pinned up the family trees.

It was fun to look at them. They found out things about each other they'd never known before.

"Your auntie keeps *snakes*?" "Never knew your dad was a copper..." "You've got a sister on TV?" "Your gran lives on a boat?"

"I know all about your mum," one of the girls told Josh.

This was it, thought Josh, cowering. Taxi! Taxi! all over again.

"Your mum picked up my cousin," said the girl. Other people came round to hear. "My big cousin was coming home late from this party, and someone stole all her money, and she was crying. Then your mum turned up in that LADYFARE cab, and she didn't ask for any money. She just took my cousin home."

"Your mum's a *taxi* driver?" exclaimed one of the boys.

"She must be really nice," said someone, "to do a thing like that."

"She's not bad," said Josh briefly. "She's OK."

Matthew asked him round after school was over. One of the guinea-pigs had just had babies.

"They're a bit boring right now," said Matthew. "But they get better later on."

"Can I still have one?" asked Josh.

"Have the six if you like," Matthew's mum offered.

"You coming to our party?" asked Josh.

"You bet," Matthew said.

Josh wondered how Matthew would get on with Damien. Having an old friend meet a new friend felt funny, he thought. A bit like having a ghost dog meeting a real dog.

It was beginning to be hard to go on thinking about a real dog.

And would the ghost dog go away if a real dog came along?

If they ever let him have one...

CHAPTER TEN

At six o'clock, as usual, they took him to the park.

They unclipped his lead and turned him loose.

He did what they brought him for. Then he sensed he was free.

He ran further into the bushes. He could hear them calling him and crashing about, but he didn't care.

He was free! He was free! He could go home.

Suddenly a bigger dog barred his way.

The bigger dog insulted him. He couldn't put up with that!

A strange woman separated them. "That's quite enough!" she bellowed. She dragged him out and gave him back to the man and the woman.

Stupid animal, they growled, putting him on a short lead. Nothing but trouble.

Nothing but mess.

He licked the scratch on his chest. He felt a bit silly.

Then he followed them, wheezing, back to the flats.

They bought bottles of wine. They bought cartons of fruit juice. They shook out crisps and salty biscuits, and made sandwiches and dips.

Mum baked a big cake which Dad turned into a house. 23 ALBERT ROAD, he iced across its roof.

"Oh, aren't you clever?" exclaimed Pat in her twinkly pink dress. "I'd never have thought of that."

Friends of Cath's arrived, and ate up all the Smarties. Then Damien's lot turned up.

"Will you look at that spread!" gasped Damien's mum.

Josh and Cath walked around with sausage rolls and dips. Pat took over Josh's tray.

"I'll do that," she said. "You go off and have fun."

Josh suddenly thought of something. "You know that dog?"

"What dog?" mumbled Pat, her mouth full of sausage roll.

"That old lady's dog."

Pat nodded, speechless.

"What was it called?"

Pat thought for a moment, then smiled.

"Gyp," she said. "Short for Gypsy. I think she called him that because he was a stray."

Gyp. It fitted. It was perfect.

Gyp, he thought, calling it, and the ghost dog appeared, floating above the bowls of nuts on the coffee table.

Josh burst out laughing.

"What's so funny?" Matthew asked.

Josh gulped back his giggles. "Just something I thought."

"Want to meet us for hurling?" asked Damien. "In your big park, next weekend?"

"What's hurling?" asked Matthew.

"It's an Irish game," Josh told him. "You play it with sticks and a small leather ball called a *sliothar*. It's wild!"

"I like new games," said Matthew. "Can I come? Can I watch?"

"Play if you want to," offered Damien. "The more, the better."

The shadow boy had suddenly called him, called him by his name.

"Gyp," he'd said. "Gyp."

Gyp understood now. The boy was his new boss.

"Gyp," he'd called, and so he had to obey.

Her downstairs room was crowded, full of shadow people.

That cat saw him, and hissed.

He'd soon sort her out...

* * *

"What's got into Mollie?" asked Mum. "Spits at nothing, then she's off like a streak of light."

"Got the wind up," said Pat. "My cat does the same."

The ghost dog faded. Josh sneaked away triumphantly. He'd found the dog's ball. Now he had the dog's name.

"Gyp!" he whispered. "Gyp!" And the ghost dog was there, in his room.

He tried throwing the ball. The dog ran after it, then stopped.

He couldn't pick it up.

Josh grinned. You needed a ghost ball for a ghost dog to play with.

Damien wandered in.

"You still got that ghost?" he asked.

Josh nodded, watching Gyp.

"I've been thinking," said Damien. "It couldn't be a dog." His voice dropped. "But maybe it's an evil spirit that's taken a dog's shape."

Josh looked at Gyp's silly face, at his earnest brown eyes. "It's just a dog," he told Damien. "Honest."

"'Thought you were getting a real one," said Damien.

"We are," said Josh. "Sometime." Gyp was still there. Could ghost dogs understand? "I'm not sure I still want one," he added quickly. "And anyway, I'm getting a guinea-pig first..."

CHAPTER ELEVEN

One day, a stranger rode up to the house in the sky, and broke open the door lock and came walking in.

He could hear the stranger moving about outside. Then he barged into the kitchen.

"They shut you up in here all day?" the stranger said. "That's no way to treat a dog!"

The stranger patted him, and stroked him, and stopped him feeling lonely. Then he opened the fridge and threw him a pork chop.

The stranger took all the woman's glittery stuff and put it in a bag. Then he picked up the video.

He missed the stranger when he left...

It was the first week of October, Josh's birthday month. The sun shone golden, but the air was cool.

Each day, Josh couldn't wait to get home

from school. He'd eat something quickly, then go out to the garden.

"What are you playing?" nagged Cath, watching him endlessly throwing the ball, running to pick it up, then throwing it down again.

"Just a game," said Josh.

"What game?" insisted Cath.

"You wouldn't understand," said Josh airily.

"Yes, I would so," snapped Cath, offended. "It's a stupid game anyway. I wouldn't want to play."

Josh didn't care. He and Gyp had worked things out. He'd throw the ball. Then Gyp would chase it. "Hold!" he'd say. Then Gyp would guard it. Then Josh would pick it up, and throw it again.

Once Gyp chased it into the middle of the bushes. Josh could see brambles growing through his tummy, and out across his tail. That day, he had to scramble to get the ball back, scratching his arms against the thorns.

"We ought to cut back those bushes," said Dad, mopping him up. "And what's so special, anyway, about that old ball?"

"Josh plays with it," sneaked Cath. "He plays with it all the time."

Dad looked puzzled. "We've got good ones," he said. "Ones that bounce. That old thing can't be much fun..."

* * *

The two baby guinea-pigs rode home in Mum's cab.

"Can I hold one?" asked Cath. "Oh, they're so sweet."

They helped Mum set up the cage, then popped the little pigs inside.

"They're your responsibility now," Mum told Josh.

"Why can't they be family?" challenged Josh. "Like you always say Mollie is?"

"I'll help," offered Cath. "I'll go shares if you like."

"Wait till you clean out their cage," warned Mum. "Then you'll be singing a different tune." Her face suddenly went funny. "Call it a practice run."

"What's that?" asked Josh.

"It means going into training for something more difficult."

Cath caught on. "You don't mean a dog?"

"A *dog*?" exclaimed Mum. "Who said anything about a dog?"

"She's got a secret," Cath said later. "You can always tell."

"She's rotten at secrets." Josh giggled . "She always gives herself away." He paused. "Do you think that's what it is? I mean, about the dog?"

"We're going to have one," groaned Cath. "I know we're going to have one." She suddenly noticed Josh's face. "You're the one who's always going on about a dog," she said. "Aren't you pleased?"

"There's nothing to be pleased about," said Josh reasonably. "I mean, we don't *know* yet, do we?"

How would Gyp get on with a real dog? Josh wondered in bed.

Would he be jealous? Would he go away?

But people could have two dogs, even three or four.

Not dogs like Gyp, though.

He whispered. "*Gyp!*" But Gyp didn't appear.

He got out of bed and threw the ball around, but still nothing happened.

Then a wind rose, rattling the skeleton creeper.

And Josh shivered, and pulled the duvet over his head.

CHAPTER TWELVE

The man and the woman banged about, making phone calls.

More strangers came and went. He cowered in a corner. Some guard dog, they sniggered. A silly-looking mutt like that?

Then he heard them quarrelling, the man's voice booming, the woman's high and weepy. Their anger filled his head. There wasn't any room left for pictures of home.

They put out no food for him that night. Maybe they'd forgotten? He tried scratching at their door, but the man came out and kicked him.

Their anger filled the flat, even when they weren't there.

He lay in his basket and made pictures of nothing. Then one day, quite suddenly, something called him again.

* * *

Gyp didn't come the next day when Josh threw the ball.

Josh tried over and over, but still nothing happened. Then rain turned the lawn into a squelchy green sponge.

He tried upstairs in his room. Cath wandered in and watched him.

"Why do you keep playing that silly game?"

"Don't know," mumbled Josh.

"Beat you at Snap?" challenged Cath.

Josh gave up. "OK..."

That night, big raindrops drummed against the window. Then thunder and lightning flash-banged and roared.

Josh got up to watch. He was scared but excited. Lightning forked violet across the sky.

Would Gyp ever come again? he wondered.

And where would he be if he never came back? Where did ghosts go when they weren't being ghosts?

And he thought about the Dog Star that got everything wrong.

But that was stupid. Stars weren't magic.

They were just big balls of gas. Everyone knew that.

Amy and Pat came round to see the guinea-pigs.

"That one's called Sally," announced Cath.

"They're both boys," corrected Josh.

"Why didn't he give you one of each?"

grumbled Cath. "Then they could have had babies."

"*Lots* and *lots* of babies," pointed out Mum.

"You could have had a guinea-pig farm," suggested Amy. "And sold them to pet shops."

"Not everyone wants a guinea-pig," said Pat.

Mollie sidled in. She sat watching in the shadows.

"Can I hold one?" asked Amy. Josh opened the cage and took one out. "Ooh," sighed Amy. "Can *we* have guinea-pigs?"

"I'll think about it," said Pat.

Cath groaned. "That's what Mum always says about having a dog."

"But dogs are useful," argued Pat. "Scare burglars away."

"Burglars wouldn't bother with us," laughed Mum.

The guinea-pig went for a walk up Amy's arm.

"It's tickly," giggled Amy, showing it off to Pat.

The little pig lost its balance, fell into Amy's lap, rolled, wriggled, righted itself, then scuttled away.

In the shadows, Mollie stiffened and prepared for the hunt.

They tried to catch the little pig, but it ran under the sideboard.

"Get it!" wailed Josh, but the little pig had already gone – scurrying through the dark cave and out into the garden.

"Grab Mollie!" shrieked Cath, but Mollie was hunting.

"I'll turn the hose on that cat!" yelled Mum. "That'll stop her in her tracks."

The little pig began grazing on dandelion and clover.

Amy started crying. "It's all my fault."

A *whoosh!* of water sent the little pig running. It scrabbled into the bushes and disappeared.

Josh was horrifed. "We've got to get him out! Some other cat might catch him."

"If we disturb him," said Pat, "it might drive him further in."

Mollie prowled, looking wounded and licking her sodden fur.

"Murderer!" yelled Josh.

"No, she's not." Mum smiled. "She's just being a cat. Anyway, she hasn't done it yet." She pointed. "See?" The little pig began nosing out of the leaves.

Then Josh saw Gyp.

At first, nothing but a wagging tail. Then the rough black fur along his back, and the honey-coloured paws, like four stout little pillars. His silly eyebrows rose above his earnest brown eyes. "This is a funny-looking ball," he seemed to be saying.

The little pig looked up and froze in terror.

Josh crept slowly forward. "Hold!" he ordered Gyp. Then he scooped up the pig. "Good boy," he said.

Cath stared at him, then giggled.

"My brother's nuts," she told them. "He thinks that guinea-pig's a dog!"

CHAPTER THIRTEEN

One morning, their anger froze into something calm and cold.

They fed him early that day.

Then they clipped the lead to his collar and took him down in the lift.

He smelt Outside again. Grass and trees and cats and other dogs. It made him feel excited. Were they taking him for a walk?

The man unlocked the garage and brought out the car. The woman opened the back door and pushed him inside.

They drove out of the city. He could smell country smells. This was a treat. Much better than the park.

He sat up very straight and watched the trees and fields flash past. Once, they'd driven him to their house in the sky. Were they driving him home?

This dog's no good, they'd tell the shadow people.

The shadow people, he remembered.

Maybe they weren't shadows if you were really there.

Maybe the boy was real. He looked real.

His ball looked real, too. They'd even played with it. And that little animal had been real. (But why would anyone care about a mousie thing like that?)

That cat was real. He thumped his tail, remembering. It had been fun to spoil her hunting when it upset his boss...

Josh bought himself a mini-Frisbee just like Matthew's.

He tried it out with Cath, but they flew it over the fence.

Cath called, "Amy! Pat!" but the house next door seemed empty.

"I'll try round the front," suggested Josh. "Their car's there. I saw it."

He knocked at Pat's door, but there was no reply. He tried again, and heard someone shuffling. Then it was opened a crack, and Pat peeped out.

Her eyes were pink and puffy, and her hair stuck up in spikes. "Hi, Josh," she said feebly. "What can I do for you?"

"I flew my Frisbee over your fence," said Josh guiltily.

Pat opened the door wide. "Come on through."

"But you're not well," said Josh.

"Headache..." Pat sighed. "Amy's with her gran, to give me some peace and quiet."

"Sorry," mumbled Josh. "I can get it some other time."

"Don't worry," said Pat. "I needed to wake up. Which reminds me," she added. "That dog you were asking about. I've got a snap of him somewhere. Want to see?"

Josh suddenly felt shivery.

"Yes, please," he said, but he really wasn't sure.

He unhooked the Frisbee from a rose-bush and flew it back to Cath. "Pat's going to show me something," he told her. "I won't be long..."

Inside, Pat was rifling through a box full of photos. "Must sort this lot out," she muttered. "Oh, look, here he is. And there's dear little Miss Nelson. And here's one of Amy in her hard hat, after her birthday ride."

But Josh didn't see Miss Nelson. He didn't notice Amy.

He was staring at his ghost dog.

He was looking at Gyp.

They picked up speed and moved on to a bigger road. He saw cars zooming past them in the fast lane.

Fast. Fast. Fast.

Home, he thought. They might soon be

there.

Slow. Slow.

They moved on to the hard shoulder, and turned off the engine. The woman opened the back door and he scrambled out. They were being nice to him today, but he still didn't like them.

They unclipped his lead, then took off his collar. He ran into the bushes to pee. He'd been a long time in the car...

Pat said, "What made you think Miss Nelson's dog had died?"

Josh went pink. "Don't know." And then he said it. "I do know really. I've seen his ghost."

"His *ghost*?" exclaimed Pat. "What does it look like?"

"A dog," said Josh. "Just a dog."

Pat was silent.

"Well, why not?" she said slowly. "Why shouldn't a dog have a ghost? If there are such things as ghosts. So he died..." She shook her head. "He was such a lively little chap."

"He died of sadness," Josh told her.

"I wouldn't be suprised," said Pat. "So where do you see him?"

"Everywhere." It was so good to tell someone. "In my room. And the garden." He grinned. "He even turned up at our party."

"Well, fancy that," giggled Pat. "After a sausage roll, I bet."

"You don't believe me," accused Josh.

Pat went serious. "No one would make up a thing like that. I mean, why bother?" She frowned. "Does he want something, d'you think?"

"What do you mean?"

"Ghosts are always supposed to be looking for something..."

"I found his ball," said Josh.

"That old thing?" gasped Pat.

Josh suddenly thought of something. "You won't tell my mum? Or my dad?"

"Not if you haven't. Promise. Cross my heart..." Pat held out the photo. "Have it, if you like."

"Can I?" breathed Josh. He slid it carefully into his pocket. "Thanks," he said.

CHAPTER FOURTEEN

He ran back.

The car had gone.

Then he panicked, running up and down the side of the motorway.

They'd spot him. Wouldn't they?

They'd come back, feeling stupid – they'd left without him.

Then they'd pick him up.

Wouldn't they?

The blue autumn day was gone, the sky had clouded over, and the first drops of heavy rain were splashing on the road.

The glittery moon-eyes of cars flashed coldly past him. He saw a gap and ran out. A van swerved, nearly hitting him.

He ran back into the bushes. His legs felt trembly.

Then he pulled himself together. Wasn't this what he'd wanted?

They'd gone. They'd left him.
Now he could find his way home...

Dad came to Miss Thompson's class to talk about pictures. Funny being at school, Josh thought, and listening to his dad.

Dad talked about colours and shapes, and showed them books he'd made pictures for. Then he passed round big sheets of paper.

"It'll be Hallowe'en soon," he told them. "That's good and spooky. How about some paintings of witches and ghosts?"

Josh had almost forgotten it was Dad – he seemed so much like a teacher. And he didn't speak to Josh much, which was only fair, Josh thought.

Josh did a witch's fire and a big black cauldron. Then he mixed some green and white, and painted skeletons and skulls. It was fun making it scary, but he knew real ghosts weren't like that.

He'd stood the photo on his shelf and scattered autumn leaves around it. Flowers would have been nicer, but there weren't any good ones left.

He wondered if they'd put Gyp into some pets' cemetery, if he might find his grave one day, and see his name on a stone: GYP.

And *had* he been looking for something? And had he found it and left?

For he had come back once, to save the

guinea-pig, and then never returned...

Josh walked back from school with Matthew. Cath and Amy tagged on behind.

"You never turned up for the hurling," Josh said.

"Changed my mind, didn't I?" Matthew shuffled through the leaves. "Couldn't play," he argued. "Anyway, I prefer football."

"How do you know?" asked Josh. "If you never play anything else?"

Matthew sighed.

"I *did* turn up," he confessed. "Then I saw all those Irish kids..."

"Only Damien and Greg," said Josh. "And some boys from Greg's club. We'd have been even," he complained, "if you'd joined in."

Matthew changed the subject. "Your dad was great," he said. "Wish I could draw like that."

"He's hopeless at games, though," said Josh. "Can't hit a ball for toffee."

"That boy Damien," Matthew remembered, "said you had a ghost."

Cath heard.

"In *our* house?" she squeaked. "Nobody told me." She turned back to Amy. "My brother's nuts," she said. "Believes in banshees."

"What's a banshee?" asked Amy.

"It's a ghost that howls," Josh told her,

"when someone's going to die."

Amy shivered. "That's scary."

"There aren't any here," said Cath. "They're only in Ireland."

"So what have you got?" asked Matthew.

"A headless lady," croaked Josh. "She walks up and down saying, '*Oo-oo-oo!*'" He leapt about, waving his arms.

"We've got a ghost, too," whispered Amy. "It's a big floating skull!"

"That's nothing," boasted Matthew. "We've got a mummy."

"Sure, everyone's got one of those," giggled Cath.

CHAPTER FIFTEEN

The bushes marked the edge of a great forest. It was twilight in there, and the rain hardly got through.

He could smell pine and rabbit and mouse. He could smell fox and badger and squirrel. The smells excited him, made him feel wild. He was free. He could run. The whole world was his.

He chased a squirrel up a tree, then ran around, barking. He followed rabbit scent and the quivering of leaves. The outside whispering of rain hushed the noise of the motorway. There was nothing now but forest. Forest and rain.

Under a sudden slit of sky, he found a ditch with muddy water. He drank, shook himself, then ran back under the trees. His coat was still wet, his whiskers damp and drooping. He nosed at a wood ant, then settled down to rest.

He was hungry, he realized. Someone really ought to feed him. But there were no people in the forest. Only rabbits and owls.

He put his head between his paws and thought about food. He closed his eyes and remembered...

His lady used to give him treats. A bone from the butcher, a little bit of fresh fish.

But his lady was gone, and the boy couldn't help.

Who wanted shadow food?

Amy came round to play with Cath.

"Oh, Josh," she said. "My mum wants to see you."

Josh felt nervous. Had he done something?

He went next door and rang the bell.

"Hi, Josh." Pat smiled. "Come on in." She opened the fridge and brought out two cans. "Orange or pineapple?"

"Pineapple, please," said Josh.

Pat suddenly got serious. "Amy's started having nightmares," she said. "About ghosts." She looked at Josh solemnly. "Was that you?"

Josh's ears went hot.

"We were fooling," he said. "And Cath told her about banshees..."

"What about your ghost dog?"

"Not that," said Josh, shocked. "Only you know about that." He corrected himself. "Damien didn't believe me."

Pat ran her fingers through her brushy blonde hair.

"We were just making things up," argued Josh. "I didn't think she'd believe us."

"Tell her ghosts aren't true," ordered Pat.

"I can't, can I?" said Josh.

Pat opened a pack of biscuits. "Are you still seeing him?"

Josh shook his head sadly. "I think he's gone away."

"He'd have had to go in the end," said Pat. "What if you got a real dog?"

"You can have two dogs, can't you?"

Pat shrugged. "I suppose you can."

He dozed, then woke up. The forest was black.

Home, he remembered.

He stretched and got up. Then he shook himself and started walking, steering between the old smells and new, picking out a track, a direction, a way through.

Suddenly lights whirled flashes of green and brown and gold. There was a bang! *and he panicked, blundering into brambles.*

Something came flapping out of the trees in a flurry of pine needles. It fell down and lay still. It smelt of bird. It smelt of blood.

Men came crackling and flashing through the bushes. Gyp snapped at them and growled, but they held him by the neck.

"Give us away, would you?" a man threatened.

"You could train that fellow," said another. "He's got the right idea."

"You want a proper dog," sneered the first man. "Not a stray mutt like that."

They dropped the dead bird into a sack. Then they put him on a rope.

"You'd better shut up and behave yourself, mate ..." they clicked a shotgun "... or you'll get some of this."

CHAPTER SIXTEEN

He stiffened his legs. The man dragged him along. The rope squeezed his throat and rubbed at his neck.

He cried because it hurt. That was when the man hit him. Better stay quiet, he thought, and feel round for escape.

They came out of the forest and into a meadow. Their torches cast little moons of light on the damp, dark grass. Gyp smelt fox, and sheep droppings, and the dead birds in the sack.

Then he picked up a new scent...

*The new people moved stealthily. His men hadn't seen them. Then all at once, a crack-*bang! *made him howl in fear. There was a flashing of torches and a jumble of voices.*

"Poachers!" someone roared. "Got 'em this time. There's a dog with them, too. I'll shoot the dirty mutt!"

He felt the man's hand slacken for a second, so he tugged and was free. He tore back into the forest, the rope trailing beside him.

A shotgun sounded CRACK! and he slunk under a bush. He lay low, listening, his chest and paws trembling. Someone crashed about near him, snapping twigs.

"I'll get him," the man was muttering. "I'll set my hounds on that mutt..."

A man called round to Josh's house just after teatime.

Mum brought him in.

"This is Ben," she said.

Ben shook Josh's hand. "So you're the boy who likes dogs."

Josh nodded, puzzled. What was it to him?

"Could I see the garden?" asked Ben, and they went outside to look.

"A dog might dig holes," Ben pointed out. "Until you trained him not to. Would anyone mind?"

"Not really," said Dad.

"You've got to walk a dog," said Ben. "Even when it's raining."

"That's OK," said Josh. "I wouldn't mind doing that."

They went back inside. Mum was looking mysterious. "You see, Ben knows someone who keeps dogs," she told him.

"What kinds of dogs?" asked Josh.

"What kind do you like best?" said Ben.

Josh thought about a mongrel with silly eyebrows. "Collies, I suppose," he said. "Like my gran's."

"How about a spaniel," said Cath, "with nice floppity ears?"

"'Thought you didn't like dogs," Josh said.

"I like some dogs," said Cath.

Ben picked up Mollie and began to stroke her.

"She's mine," said Cath. "I found her when she was a kitten."

Ben sighed. "Cats sometimes give dogs problems. They can be really mean."

Cath exploded. "But dogs chase cats!"

"And cats scratch dogs," Ben told her. "It doesn't usually last, though, once they get to be friends..." He walked over to the cage. "And whose are the guinea-pigs?"

"They're mine," said Josh.

"I think you've got enough pets," said Ben, getting up. "But if you'd like to see my friend's dogs, I could arrange it for you one day."

Gyp, thought Josh in bed that night.

"Gyp!" he called softly, holding out the ball.

He'd almost forgotten about wanting a real dog. Then Mum had put on her "secrets" face and Ben had turned up.

She was plotting something. Cath had

been quite sure.

A real dog would be great, but Gyp had been so special.

A real dog you could stroke, though, and fool around with. A real dog would chase sticks and bring them back.

But would Gyp be jealous if they got a real dog?

But Gyp wasn't around any more, remembered Josh.

CHAPTER SEVENTEEN

He woke up. He'd been dreaming of rabbits.

He stretched, and brambles caught at his rope. He tore himself free, and picked his way out. He was hungry, he was thirsty and he ached all over.

The sun had just risen, a small bright smudge on the watery grey cloud. A mist blurred the edges of the pale, damp meadow. He licked at wet leaves, then started to walk.

The forest petered out and turned into a track. He followed the track till it turned into a lane. He followed the lane till he came to some houses. Then he walked through back gardens and came out on a street.

It was dustbin day and the black bags were bulging. Foxes had already been and gone, but there was plenty left for him. A dawn cat spat at him, but he ignored her. He could smell chicken and chop bones and empty dog-food tins.

He tore open a bag and its goodies oozed out. A can went clanking and rattling across the pavement.

Someone banged open a window. "Get out of it!" yelled a voice.

So he moved on. There were other bags to raid.

He found a half-eaten chicken, and settled down to finish it. A puddle on a dustbin lid gave him water to drink. Starlings whirled in the sky above his head. He licked his whiskers clean. He felt pleased with himself.

He was trying to reach his sore place when the newspaper boy pedalled past on his bike.

The boy braked and turned back. "You're a stray!" he yelled. "Worse than foxes!" He dumped his bike and made a grab, but missed...

Josh rang Damien.

"We're going to a McDonald's for my birthday," he said. "Can you come?"

"You mean, on Wednesday?" asked Damien.

"No, on Saturday," said Josh.

"Isn't Wednesday your birthday?"

"Yes," said Josh. "But they've planned something for Wednesday."

"What?" Damien asked.

"How would I know?" said Josh.

Josh asked Matthew and Robbie.

"My real birthday's on Wednesday," he told them. "But I'm having a treat."

He kept wondering what it was.

Even Cath was wearing a "secrets" face now.

"You know something," Josh said.

"But I'm not telling," simpered Cath.

"Give me a clue," begged Josh.

Cath frowned. "It just might," she said slowly, "be something to do with a visitor..."

That man Ben, thought Josh. He'd talked about a friend who kept dogs. Maybe they'd let him choose one. Maybe then he'd forget Gyp.

Who wanted a ghost dog?

He did, he thought, picking up the snapshot.

"Gyp," he called softly, but no ghost dog appeared. Gyp, he thought. Are you sulking because they might get me a real dog? But people can love two dogs. My grammie does.

But then Grammie's dogs were real dogs, remembered Josh.

He was travelling again.

He would have preferred to have rested with his nice, full tummy, but he needed to get right away from that boy.

And there were new scents in the air, new clues to follow. He picked out heather and tar and fox and pheasant. He picked out cows and sheep. The sheep smell made him quiver.

He ducked under a wire fence and ran into a field. The white woolly things baa-ed and started running. They didn't run fast, and it was fun to scare them. He didn't hear the van, didn't spot the two men running across the grass until one of them grabbed him and held him down.

The man picked him up and carried him back to the van. He crouched, growling, in the back, behind the bars.

Just before they slammed the door, he caught a whiff of the other smell.

Salt. Sea. One of the sweet smells of home.

So he'd nearly made it...

He shook his head in despair, and began to howl.

CHAPTER EIGHTEEN

He hurled himself, hopelessly, against the metal grid.

One of the men called out, "Easy, boy."

He saw the road through the windscreen, hedges and trees flying past, all the ground he'd covered winding itself back.

He crouched, defeated.

Then he closed his eyes.

He remembered the warm quilt on his lady's bed.

Home, he thought sadly.

And the boy he couldn't touch reached out and tried to stroke him...

Josh always woke up early on the morning of his birthday.

On Wednesday it was dawn, and there was Gyp.

"Oh, Gyp!" he whispered, reaching out. "Have you come back to wish me a happy birthday?" He climbed out of bed and picked up the ball. "Fetch it, boy!" he urged, but Gyp didn't move.

Then Josh snuggled down beside him on the bed. "You're sad, aren't you?" he said. He tried to stroke Gyp's head, knowing he couldn't. "Are you jealous?" he asked. Gyp gazed at him sorrowfully. "Listen," Josh told him. "You'll always be my best dog, even though you're just a ghost."

He lay, looking at Gyp, until Gyp wasn't there. Then he drifted into an early morning dream.

Cath crashed into it, bouncing on his bed.

"Happy birthday!" she yelled.

"Thanks," mumbled Josh.

He got dressed and went down to look at his cards. There was one from Matthew, and one from Damien. Grammie O'Keefe had sent a dog card, and there was a glittery cut-out rocket from Gran and Grandpa Roberts.

"Don't forget," Mum told them before they left for school, "we're picking you both up at three." She gave them each a note. "Be sure your teachers let you out early..."

In the afternoon, they hung about in the playground with First Year Infants and their mums.

Cath was wriggling with excitement. "Just you wait," she told Josh.

Then Mum sounded the horn on the LADY-FARE cab.

"There they are!" squeaked Cath. "Come on! Come on!"

Mum drove them up through the town and out into the country.

"You excited?" asked Cath.

"You bet," said Josh.

But he wasn't excited. He was sad.

He kept seeing Gyp's face, and remembering his promise. And what if this friend of Ben's had a dog he really liked?

They drove through lanes and out on to a smaller road.

"That's the turning," said Dad. "That's it, Josh. We're here." And he pointed at the sign: HAZELMERE DOGS' HOME.

They scrunched up the drive and parked round the side. Josh still couldn't believe it, even though he'd worked it out. "You mean, I can choose a dog from here?"

"If you still want one," grinned Dad.

"Remember Ben?" Mum told him as they all got out. "Well, Ben works here. And he needed to check us out – that's why he came round. They don't let just anyone have one of their dogs."

They went into the office and found Ben waiting.

"Happy birthday," he said. Then he noticed Josh's face. "You don't look much like a birthday boy," he said. "Are you quite sure you still want one of our dogs?"

They walked round to the kennels. The noise was deafening.

"All looking for families," Ben told them. "Isn't it sad?" He reached in and patted a golden retriever. "Imagine anyone not wanting a dog like this!" He turned to Josh. "Just take your time. No hurry. Come back tomorrow if you like, or even next week. A dog's got to be right. It's like choosing a friend."

They walked round. They looked.

"Let's have a collie," said Cath. "You're always saying you like collies."

"I fancy this little fellow," said Mum.

"It's for Josh to choose," Dad reminded them. "After all, it's Josh's birthday. And it's going to be his dog."

"Not a family dog?" asked Cath slyly. "Like Mollie's a family cat?"

"We all love Mollie," snapped Mum, "but we all know she's yours."

Ben touched Josh's shoulder. "Why not go round by yourself? If you listen to this lot, you'll want every dog in the place!"

"But I do already," wailed Josh. It was really happening, he thought. These were real dogs, not ghost dogs, and one of them could be his.

Collies were the best, he thought. He loved playing with Grammie's. He pointed at a black and white one, and Ben brought him out.

"Oh, you're beautiful," said Josh. (But would Gyp be jealous?)

"There's an exercise place over there. See?" Ben pointed. "Take him along. Get to know each other..."

CHAPTER NINETEEN

Ben picked up a stick.

"Try him on this," he told Josh.

The collie raced after it, then attacked it, growling. Josh grabbed one end and pulled, like he did with Grammie's dogs. The collie let go, and he fell over on the grass.

He giggled and got up, then suddenly felt Gyp's presence, as if the ghost dog was watching them with his sad, chestnut eyes. It wasn't much fun being a ghost dog, thought Josh. Like always looking through a window, watching other people play.

He gave the stick to Ben. "You throw it this time," he said. He wandered over to an enclosure behind the two big rows of kennels. "What's in here?" he asked.

Ben smiled. "That's where we put our newcomers. They turn up frightened and confused, often ill-treated. They need a day or two at least to be by themselves..." He pointed at a huddle of fur curled up inside a shelter. "Take that little chap. Found him worrying sheep this morning. No collar. A stray. Farmer might have shot him if we hadn't spotted him first."

Josh shivered. "Can I see him?"

"Not now," said Ben, throwing the stick for the collie. "That fellow needs to rest. Then he's got to have his jabs."

The collie worried at the stick. Then he brought it back and dropped it. Play with me, play with me, he barked.

But Josh couldn't take his eyes off the sad bundle of fur.

Gyp might not be jealous of a dog that looked like that.

"Come here, boy," he said softly.

The bundle shifted, then settled.

"Come on," Josh urged. It suddenly seemed to matter.

He felt someone calling him, and knew it was the boy.

He shifted and turned and opened one eye.

Then he stared, puzzled. This wasn't home.

Yet there was his shadow boy, looking through the fence.

He rolled over. He was tired, he was sore, and he wanted to go home. The van people had been kind, but they'd still locked him up.

The boy was calling him again. Why

couldn't he let him sleep?

He turned his head and looked. The boy seemed different. Solid. Real.

He could even smell him. The boy smelt so good...

He stretched and got up slowly.

Then he went over to investigate.

It was Gyp!

But that was silly. Gyp was dead. How else could you come to be a ghost?

The dog began licking Josh's fingers.

"Oh, Gyp," whispered Josh. He just couldn't help it.

"Gyp?" he repeated.

The dog raised his silly eyebrows.

"Gyp?" Josh yelled, and the dog thumped his tail.

"Gyp!" Josh shouted. The dog scrabbled at the railings.

Ben looked puzzled. "Do you know him?"

"*Know* him?" Josh stood up. "It's Gyp! He's the dog who used to live in our house, before we moved in."

"Then you must know his owner." Ben looked fierce. "Not that he deserves a dog."

"His owner died," said Josh quickly. "That's how Gyp got to be a stray."

Ben unlocked the enclosure.

"This is against our rules, you know," he said, as Josh slipped inside. "We like to leave new dogs in peace. But you two seem made for each other..." He grinned down at the tangle of boy and dog. "Do you want him, then?"

"What do you think?" gasped Josh, tickling Gyp's tummy.

"You'll have to wait," Ben told him. "You can't take him now. Even if it is your birthday."

"That's OK."

"And he's only a mongrel," Ben teased. "Not in the same class as this handsome chap."

Josh looked at the collie. "He's beautiful," he agreed. "But you see, I've already got a dog..."

They pushed four tables together at McDonalds on Saturday.

They ate hamburgers and chips and strawberry ice-cream.

"But what's this dog like?" persisted Damien.

"Can I come round tomorrow," asked Matthew, "to see?"

"You should have seen the one he didn't get," sighed Cath. "A lovely black and white collie..."

"But Gyp's special," Josh told them.

Pat stared at him. "Is that his name?"

"He looks a bit like that old lady's dog," said Josh.

"Maybe he didn't die," murmured Pat.

"Who didn't?" asked Amy.

"Someone we knew once." Pat smiled at Josh. "So you won't be needing that photo..."

"What photo?" asked Cath.

"Secrets," Pat told her.

"Tell," begged Amy.

But then the birthday cake arrived, and they all forgot.

CHAPTER TWENTY

The boy came back for him.

Gyp was scared he'd gone for ever, like his lady had.

The boy fastened a new collar around his neck. "You're mine, now," he said. Well, Gyp knew that.

Cars still felt scary, but the boy stroked and soothed him. Then Gyp smelt his old street and began to dribble.

They stopped outside a house.

The boy let him out and he ran up the path. They unfastened the door and Gyp pushed his way in. He went all over the place. It smelt good. It smelt right.

Then the cat that wasn't a shadow spat at him and hissed.

Gyp didn't care. He could handle cats.

He went outside and ran in happy circles through the grass.

"Hi, Gyp!" called the big, blonde lady with the nice, familiar smell.

"Come on, boy!" yelled his boss, and Gyp leapt up and licked his face.

It was great to be home.